D0116609

Badness for Beginners

A Little Wolf and Smellybreff Adventure

For Teddy and Ella—
who never get spoilt rotten, hem hem—
with love from You-Know-Who.

—I.W.

First American edition published in 2005 by Carolrhoda Books, Inc.

Text copyright © 2005 by Ian Whybrow
Illustrations copyright © 2005 by Tony Ross

Published by arrangement with HarperCollins Publishers Ltd., London, England. Originally published in English by HarperCollins Publishers Ltd. under the title Little Wolf and Smellybreff: Badness for Beginners .

The author and artist assert the moral right to be identified as the author and artist of this work.

Carolrhoda Books, Inc.
A division of Lerner Publishing Group
241 First Avenue North
Minneapolis, MN 55401 U.S.A.

Website address: www.carolrhodabooks.com

Library of Congress Cataloging-in-Publication Data
Whybrow, Ian.
Badness for beginners : a Little Wolf and Smellybreff adventure / by
Ian Whybrow ; illustrated by Tony Ross.— 1st American ed.
p.   cm.
Summary: Little Wolf and his brother Smellybreff get a lesson in
Badness from Mom and Dad.
ISBN: 1–57505–861–8 (lib. bdg. : alk. paper)
[1. Wolves—Fiction. 2. Behavior—Fiction. 3. Brothers—Fiction.
4. Parent and child—Fiction.] I. Ross, Tony, ill. II. Title.
PZ7.W6225Bag 2005
[Fic]—dc22   2004027720

Printed and Bound in Singapore
1 2 3 4 5 6 – OS – 10 09 08 07 06 05

Badness for Beginners

A Little Wolf and Smellybreff Adventure

Ian Whybrow + Tony Ross

Carolrhoda Books, Inc./Minneapolis

In a nice smelly lair, far away, lived the Wolf family.
There was Mom Wolf, Dad Wolf, Little Wolf, and Baby Wolf.
(He was the smelliest, so they called him Smellybreff.)

Mom and Dad were very proud of being
BIG and BAD. They wanted Little and Smellybreff
to grow up big and bad like them.

Mom and Dad taught the cubs naughty nursery rhymes.

Their favorite was "Never Say Thank You."

Never say thank you
Play with your food
Make all your noises
Naughty and rude
Talk with your mouth full
Answer back quick
Never stop eating
till you feel sick

Smellybreff was a
quick learner—he was
full of Badness.

But sometimes, Little
was good by
mistake.

One day, Mom and Dad decided to teach Little and Smells more about Badness. Off they went to town.

"Remember," said Dad, "you must both be on your WORST behavior."

The Wolf family came to a bridge that was being repaired.
Dad said, "Watch me!"

He went, "GRRR!" and
scared the workers away.

He kicked over their
danger sign.

He kicked over their
warning lights.

And, he ate their
sandwiches.

Mom said, "Good job, dear!
That was very big and bad!
What a fine example
you are to the cubs!"

Smellybreff wanted to be big and bad like his dad.
But Little said, "No, Smells, you are only
a baby. Watch me!"

He made a mud pie in the road.
(It wasn't a very bad thing to do,
but Little was trying his hardest.)

Smellybreff went
screamy-scream.

BRRRR

Then he jumped on the
workers' drill and went...

BRRRRRRRBRRRRRRRR... BRRRRRRRR... BRRRRRRRRRRRRR... BRRRRRRRRRRRRRR... BRRRRRR... BRRRRRRBRRRRRRRRRR...

Soon there was a BIG hole.

"Well done, Smells!" said Mom. "What a clever cub!"

"For your next Badness lesson,"
said Dad, "we'll go to the café."

"Thanks, Dad!" said Little.

"Grrr!" said Dad. "Stop being so polite,
Little! Why can't you learn to misbehave?"

At the café, Little tried really hard to be bad. Out went his tongue—wiggle, wiggle.

"Poor little cubby, you must be thirsty," said the waitress.

She patted him on the head and gave him a nice cold milk shake.

Smells went screamy-scream until he got a milk shake too. He swallowed it in one gulp.

Then he went . . .

BBUURPPPP! BBBBBBBBBB

"Good job, darling baby!" said Mom
and Dad. "That was very bad."

"I will try being bad one more time!" said Little.

He jumped up and went, "Grrr!"

"Oh, what a lovely smile, little cubby!" said the waitress.

She patted him on the head and gave him a dog biscuit.

Smellybreff was still hungry. He ate four banana splits and a giant hot fudge sundae.

Then he threw up on the floor.
"What a smart cub!" said Mom.

Along came the waitress with a bucket
of soapy water to clean up the mess.
Out went Smellybreff's naughty tail.

WHOOPS!

went the waitress.

SLOSH! went the water. Everyone got soaked.

"GET OUT!" shouted the waitress. "Go away, you BAD animals and never-ever-ever come back!" She chased them all the way to the bridge.

By then it was getting dark.
There was no danger sign.
There were no warning lights.

"AAAH!" went Mom,
as she tripped on
Little Wolf's mud pie.

"WHOAAA!" went Dad,
as he fell through the
hole that Smellybreff
had made.

Dad crawled back onto the bridge.

Little said, "Aren't we good at being BAD, Dad?
Smellybreff made a big hole in the road. And my
mud pie made Mom trip and knock you down the hole."

Back at the lair, Little said, "We learned
a lot about Badness today, Mom and Dad!
Will you teach us more tomorrow, please?"

All Mom and Dad could say was,

"GRRR!"

So Little howled this naughty lullaby
to make Mom and Dad feel better:

Hushabye, wolf cub,
Please do not snore—
Or I will shut your
Tail in the door.
Mommy and Daddy
Both need a rest.
Wait till tomorrow—
Then be a pest!

And that gave Smellybreff a very bad idea...